Goat's Goal

by Mindy Menschell
illustrated by Sam Day

Harcourt

Orlando   Boston   Dallas   Chicago   San Diego

Crow, Toad, and Goat lived
by a lake. They had never gone
to the other side.

One day, Goat said, "Let's set a goal. We will go to the other side of the lake."

"Oh, no!" groaned Crow. "I will not leave home!"

"Oh, no!" moaned Toad. "I am too old to go!"

"Then I will go alone," said Goat.
She got into her boat and began
to row. But . . .

Goat's boat would not float.
Goat got soaked!

"I will swim," said Goat. So
Goat began to swim. But ...

Goat was very slow. Goat's
toes got too cold!

"I will go on the road," said
Goat. So she put on her coat
and walked down the road.
And . . .

Goat reached the other side.
Goat was very glad. She waved
to Crow and Toad.

Crow and Toad saw Goat.
"Let's try to go, too," said Crow.
"I can fly with a load. Hop on
my back and hold on."

Crow and Toad landed.
"Now I know," Goat told them,
"that if I keep trying, I can
reach my goal!"